ALADDIN

Louis Weber, C.E.O.
Publications International, Ltd.
7373 North Cicero Avenue
Lincolnwood, Illinois 60646

Manufactured in U.S.A.

8 7 6 5 4 3 2 1

ISBN: 0–7853–1024–X

Cover Illustration by Tim Huhn

Illustrations by Gary Torrisi

Contributing Writer: Bette Killion

PUBLICATIONS INTERNATIONAL, LTD.

Aladdin was a poor boy who lived in a small house just outside the city. He made his living by gathering dry sticks and selling them for kindling at the market.

One day, Aladdin loaded his bundle of sticks on his back and walked to the city. Amir, his pet mongoose, rode on his shoulder, looking alertly around him. There were many wondrous sights to see in the city.

That day, a great, bustling crowd filled the marketplace. Suddenly, a cry rang out, "Make way! Make way! The sultan's daughter, Princess Lylah, is coming through!"

The princess rode on a splendid white horse with her royal court around her. Aladdin pushed to the front of the crowd to get a glimpse of her. She was beautiful!

Amir saw the princess, too. He began chattering so loudly that the princess turned and smiled at him. Aladdin's heart filled with love for her.

Standing in the crowd near Aladdin was a clever magician named Rasheed. He looked Aladdin up and down for a moment and said, "Young man, I need your help. I will give you a gold coin if you will do a simple job for me."

Aladdin followed Rasheed out into the desert. They walked a long way. At last they came to a place between two mountains.

"Here," said Rasheed. He pointed to a great rock, and Aladdin saw an opening just below it. "I cannot fit through the cave entrance, but you can. Climb down into the cave and bring me the lamp you will find there. Hurry!"

Aladdin slid into the cave. There he found heaping piles of precious jewels, and the lamp in a corner. He was about to hand it out to the magician when Amir chattered loudly and jerked his sleeve.

"Hand it out to me!" shrieked Rasheed angrily, but Aladdin refused.

Rasheed was so angry he shoved a big stone over the entrance and went away. Aladdin filled all his pockets with the precious stones. Then, with the lamp on his lap, he sat down to think. Amir ran around and around, trying to find a way out, but there was none. Aladdin began to cry.

His tears rolled down onto the lamp, and Aladdin rubbed them away. As he did, a huge genie appeared beside him.

"What do you wish of me, Master?" the genie asked in a deep, rumbling voice.

Aladdin said, "Get us out of here!"

No sooner had Aladdin spoken than he and Amir were outside the cave. He still held the lamp. He felt his pockets to make sure that he still had the precious jewels. Clutching his treasures, he ran all the way home.

Back home again, Aladdin felt hungry. He rubbed the lamp and asked the genie to bring him food. Immediately his table was spread with food fit for the sultan, all served on elegant platters. The food was delicious, but Aladdin could not eat much. His heart was aching for the sultan's beautiful daughter.

He asked the genie to outfit him in royal clothes and give him a noble horse. Then Aladdin rode to the sultan's palace. On his saddle he carried the precious stones from the cave.

The sultan's palace was huge and very impressive. Aladdin trembled at the sight, but his love for the princess carried him on.

"Sire," he said when he knelt before the sultan. "I bring you these humble jewels and ask your daughter's hand in marriage."

The sultan had never before seen such rich jewels. He thought Aladdin must be the son of a powerful sultan from another country. So he agreed to give him Princess Lylah as his wife. Lylah was pleased with this, for she thought Aladdin was a kind and handsome young man.

Aladdin and the princess were married, and the genie built them a palace even more beautiful than the sultan's palace. Aladdin and Lylah were happy there until the day Rasheed learned about what had happened to Aladdin. The magician knew Aladdin must have the magic lamp.

He hurried to a shop and bought a dozen shiny copper lamps. One day, when Aladdin was not home, Rasheed disguised himself as a peddler and brought the lamps to the palace.

"New lamps for old!" he called. The princess, remembering Aladdin's battered old lamp, decided to surprise him with a new one. The sly magician gladly traded one of his shiny lamps for the magic one. He summoned the genie right away.

"Build me a splendid palace in another city," Rasheed commanded, "and bring me Princess Lylah."

At once it was done.

Aladdin returned to his palace to find that his beloved princess was gone. Poor Aladdin! His heart was broken. But Amir slipped away and began to search for her.

For days the little mongoose searched. At last, hungry and exhausted, he came to Rasheed's palace. There he found Princess Lylah. She was sobbing for Aladdin. When Amir crept up into her lap she kissed him and tied her silk scarf around his neck.

The brave little mongoose hurried back to his master. When Aladdin saw the scarf, he recognized it right away.

"You've found my beloved Lylah, Amir," he said. "Now it's up to me to rescue her!"

Aladdin followed Amir to Rasheed's palace. They slipped through a side door and found the magic lamp while the wicked magician was sleeping. The genie was overjoyed to see Aladdin. He did not like serving the evil Rasheed. In a wink, the genie of the lamp returned Aladdin, Princess Lylah, and Amir to their own palace.

When the sultan heard the story he was very angry. He banished the evil Rasheed to a country far, far away, never to be heard from again. Aladdin, the princess, and the faithful Amir lived long and happily after that, with a little help from the genie!